S0-AWA-622

DATE DUE

**Disc
Enclosed**

AVON PUBLIC LIBRARY
BOX 977 / 200 BENCHMARK RD.
AVON, COLORADO 81620

THIS IS THE HOUSE THAT JACK BUILT

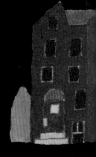

Paradise Found-beautiful post & beam Farmhse on approx. 51+ magnificent acs. Lovely level land w/lrg pond stocked with fish. This 4 BR, 2.5 bth, 2 fpl house is nestled amongst flowering trees, shrubs & perennials. Anderson French wood AC's open to decks in almost every room—truly unique. What views! What wildlife abounds! Seen by appt only. Please call listing agt Elisa Sumner 277-5000

SIMPLY ELEGANT
Beautifully sited on prime 19 acres in the heart of Bedford. Glamorous shingle style 6000+ sf of quality construction. Oversized living room w/fpl. Enormous gourmet's kitchen. Lavish master suite w/sitting room, fpl &

STUNNING CONTEMPORARY
Architect designed & set on over 3 acs of prof'lly landscpd seclusion in Lewisboro. Magnificent dropped LR w/20' ceil, formal DR, sunlit kit adj solarium b'fast room which leads to outside liv spaces & spa. 3 fpls, 2-story office/studio w/sep entrance. Winter views of

ENTIRE 4 STORY TOW
W/PRIVATE 1,000 SQ FT O
Steps to Central Pk, 5th & M
shopping. Turn of the centu
4BR's, 4 full baths & 2 pow
Sep maid's quarters or per

18th Century Manor House
Historically-significant, meticulously-restored 15-rm brick Georgian on 6+ acres. Prof'l kitch, elegant bths, new mechanicals. 19th C caretaker's wing. Ask $1,100,000
M. Woods bkr

Architect Designed
On a quiet lane, this spectacular home faces south and draws wonderful light overlooking 4 beautiful acres. 2-story cathedral ceiling center hall; fireplaces

EXTRAORDINARY FARM. Early saltbox-style house w/scrnd porch, deck, many improves. 124 rolling acres with fenced horse pastures, hayfields, woods. Small barn w/apt above, hug

Palenville Gorgeous Esca
fpl, 3BR, full bsmt, fab se
Woodstock, state preser
$597.5K Greene County Rlty

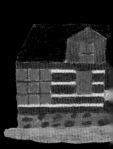

C. 1800 CENTER HALL COLONIAL 5000 sf brick. Wide CH with Palladian window. Exquisite detail: 15 rms, 5 fplcs, 5 baths. Guest house with fplc. 2 artist's studios. 3-car gar. Barn. Shop. Multi-lines & LAN for home profession. Ancient trees and organic gardens everywhere. Long tree-lined drive. Wonderful country estate. . . .$1.085M.
COLDWELL BANKER

UNDERSTATED ELEGANCE
Located on open Long Island sound and sited on a gentle rise this gracious custom bit in 1956, and sits majestically on 1.3 acres of premier waterfront property. The unobstructed views encompass Larchmont Harbor, umbrella point & the sound. The well maintained interior boasts a large living rm with fireplace and bay window flanked by doors to the patio.

A COUNTRY JEWEL
Fabulous country contemporary with exquisite gardens & decks galore. 3 BRs, 3 baths & fplc. Totally secluded on 6 acres. Priced to sell quickly. $295,000.
GITLHAM PROPERTIES

BREATHTAKING
"Nap
esque" views in a seclud
setting. Glass & log w/soar
& massive stone fplc. 40x4
building. 9+ acres of paradis
FLEMMING REAL

COUNTRY QUIET
One look at this sprawling 6BR, 3.5Bth Contemp. framed by mature trees & specimen plantings on 1.40acs in desired estate area & you'll be hooked on country life. Custom blt for lavish entertain/comfortable family living, this 15yr "young" residence boasts vaulted

ATTRACTIVE PRICE
Redecorated decor, refinished flrs & new KIT appliances. Set on almost .5 acre in a most convenient location. 4BDs, 3.5bths, LR w/fpl, DR, KIT w/ breakfast area opens to deck, Master w/whirlpool bth, lower level Rec room w/wet bar,

EXTRA SPECIAL
41 Winthrop Dr...One of Riverside's most desirable streets, renov. Colonial, state-of-art kitchen & fam. rm, 4BRs, 2.5bths, a/c, CB#GFP5075 . . . .$1,625,000
Eileen O'Connor eves 203-869-7

SUNDAY 1-3PM
Lovely old & charming Colonial in
Huntswood area, feat 4BR's, 2 ba
EIK, LR/fpl, hdwd flrs, wond htd p
new heating systm, 2-car gar & priv
Near train, bus & shops. $349,
dir:Cross County Prkwy to Grama
to #11 Ridgeway Street

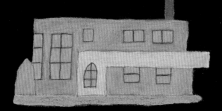

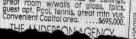

...LY RUSHING STREAM to beau-
...ountry pond. Age-old trees, rock
...ppings & old stone walls. The
...ssential country setting! 4 pic-
...ook acs. Beautifully renovated
...ry hse with slate hrdwd flrs &
...erful open flr plan by award-win-
...uilder. Dramatic Great Rm with
... Dining Area with magnificent
...Octagonal Sun Rm. Cntry Kit. 1st
...BR Ste. Guest Ste with Fpl. Office.
...l BR. Gar with Studio . .$1,450,000

AWARD-WINNING HOME...impeccab-
le design, superior materials & the
finest workmanship. State-of-art kit.
5BRs. 6F/2Hbths, MBR Suite w/fpl &
prvt deck. Indr & outdr pools. 2.25 flat
acres w/stone walls & prof lndscping.
See Virtual Tour @coldwellbanker.com
CB#NCN0443 ....$2,395,000
COLDWELL BANKER

RENOVATED FARMHOUSE
Bright, light, spacious. 4 or 5 BRs, 3 full
BAs, lrg eat-in country Kit. Great yard
with   bulbs,   perennials,   flowering
shrubs & trees, babbling brook. Worth
the ride. $199,000.

MAGNIFICENT CONTEMPORARY
Private 5 BR, 3 bath has 20' ceilings,
great room w/walls of glass, fplcs,
guest apt. Pool, tennis, great mtn vus.
Convenient Capital area. ...$695,000.
THE ANDERSON AGENCY

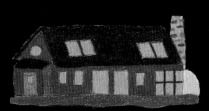

NCH MANOR HOME
cturally distinctive w/European
. Stone residence superbly set
a pretty courtyard enjoys pri-
f 4+ ac in prestigious Waccaby-

Stone Ridge. Charming country house
secluded on 20 acres. Built 1920's w/new
addition in brick. 8 BRs, 6 fplcs.
on 6./ ac. Elegant, spacious 1600s stone
house w/kingsboard flrs, FPs in LR &
DR. Sep cottage o'looks inground pool
& hot tub. Pond + stream nr paddock.
Reduced: $449,000.

PACKED WITH POTENTIAL
Comfortable and quality are just two
of the many words that will come to
mind when you see this ranch style
residence. Set on a deep lot, this 2
bedroom, 2 bath house has a large
living room, a heated solarium, an
inviting eat-in kitchen and central air

Gracious New Rocking Chair from
Porch Farmhouse Colonial set on 3.25
acs. bordered by Connecticut reservoir
land. Double height foyer w/beautiful
curved staircase, LR/Mrble Fpl, DR
Fam Rm/Fpl, Custom EIK w/Butler's

...rmo. 212-723-4340; 845-738-8229
ACEFUL COUNTRY RETREAT
SANT   VALLEY.   On   Scenic
Prop. c. 1840, 4 BR, 3000 SF
nse. Overlook ponds, fields—just
P, $2000/mo + utils.
mbia County

www.columbiacountryhomes.com
ROMANTIC HIDEAWAY
Charming 3BR 1950's cottage. LR with
FP, hdwd flrs. Spectacular 10 ac setting,
huge pond, glorious gardens, wildflow-
er meadow. Totally private, totally
wonderful. $299,000.
http://www.oldahent.com

Impeccable Cape w/sep in-law suite,
very flex flr plan, LR/fpl, DR/blt-ins,
new kit, FR w/slider to deck. 3 BRs +
den, 3.1bths. In law suite, kit, LR w/fpl
stairs to MBR w/fpl & Jacuzzi. Low
taxes on cul-de-sac. Close to town.
NEW LISTING $599,000.
Young 4BR, 2.5bth Col on luscious lvl
prop. Updated & tastefully decorat-
ed. The cntry kit w/fpl

SIMPLY ELEGANT
Beautifully sited on prime 19 acres in
the heart of Bedford. Glamorous
shingle style 6000+ sf of quality con

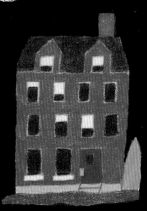

g gracious Pre-Rev. Farmhse, blt
top estate area, 3.20ac, quiet cntry
min to RR & shops; artist studio
ge. DIR: I-684N, X4, L on Rte 172, L
rles St, R on Byram Lake Rd, 1st
l, #266. CB#BEF1811

STEP INTO THE PAST! Circa 1860
Farmhouse. Beautifully proportioned
rms & period details. Hrdwd flrs, 2 Fpls,
wonderful ceiling height. Formal DR
with fabulous millwork. LR & FamRm
with Fpls. Gourmet Kit with Butler's
Pantry. Exceptional MBR Suite with
custom built-ins & Bth. 4BRs. Central
air. John Jay Schools. Walk to the re-
servation. Just listed!

www.hichenerealestate.com
WOODSTOCK area. Secluded contemp
on 6+ acres w/glorious views. Cathedral LR/fplc. 2 BRs, 2 baths. Screened
porch, deck, inground pool. $350,000.
Call Gale @ Eichhorn R.E.

MAGNIFICENT TOWNHOUSE
Grand lifestyle steps to the park! Eleg
4sty brnstn, parlor/gdn duplx. Custom
kit,fine mahogany,grand LR,deck &
gdn + 2 hi inc rntls. Xlnt cond $1,425,000

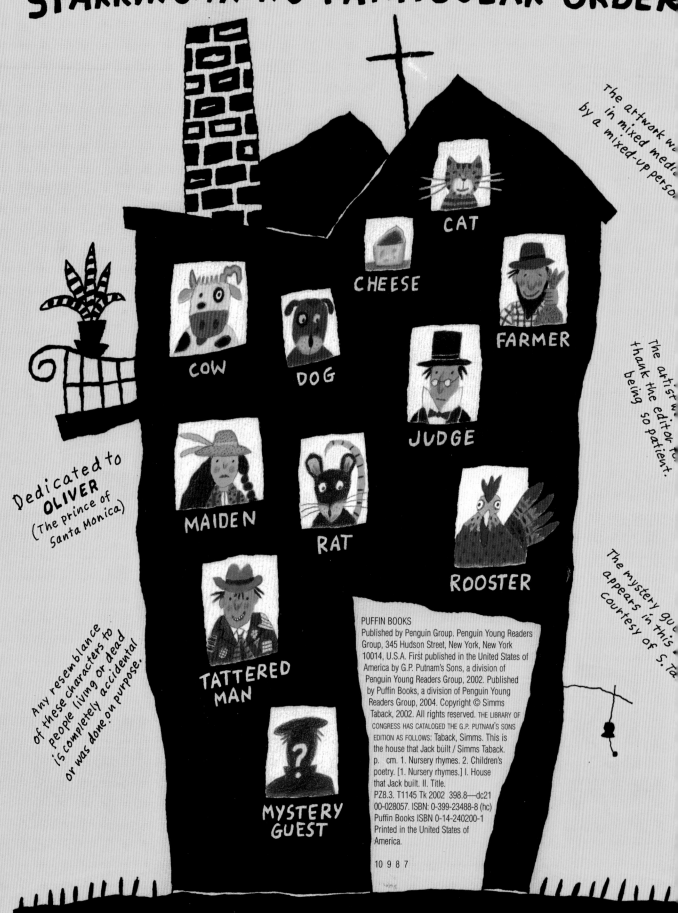

STARRING IN NO PARTICULAR ORDER

CAT

CHEESE

FARMER

COW

DOG

JUDGE

MAIDEN

RAT

ROOSTER

TATTERED MAN

MYSTERY GUEST

The artwork we in mixed medi by a mixed-up perso

The artist w thank the editor to being so patient.

The mystery gue appears in this Courtesy of S. Ta

Dedicated to **OLIVER** (The prince of Santa Monica)

Any resemblance of these characters to people living or dead is completely accidental or was done on purpose.

PUFFIN BOOKS
Published by Penguin Group. Penguin Young Readers Group, 345 Hudson Street, New York, New York 10014, U.S.A. First published in the United States of America by G.P. Putnam's Sons, a division of Penguin Young Readers Group, 2002. Published by Puffin Books, a division of Penguin Young Readers Group, 2004. Copyright © Simms Taback, 2002. All rights reserved. THE LIBRARY OF CONGRESS HAS CATALOGED THE G.P. PUTNAM'S SONS EDITION AS FOLLOWS: Taback, Simms. This is the house that Jack built / Simms Taback. p.   cm. 1. Nursery rhymes. 2. Children's poetry. [1. Nursery rhymes.] I. House that Jack built. II. Title.
PZ8.3. T1145 Tk 2002 398.8—dc21
00-028057. ISBN: 0-399-23488-8 (hc)
Puffin Books ISBN 0-14-240200-1
Printed in the United States of America.

10 9 8 7

This Is The House That Jack Built

Simms Taback

PUFFIN BOOKS

FOR
SALE

Call
Jack
for key

THIS IS THE HOUSE THAT JACK BUILT.

PLANS FOR JACK'S HOUSE
Make this bigger!
KIDS
KITCHEN
DINING

THIS IS THE CHEESE

smelly

CHEDDAR

Not so smelly

GOUDA

A little sme

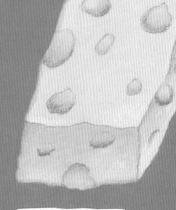
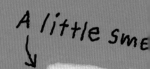

SWISS

stinky

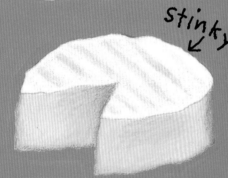

CAMEMBERT

yummy

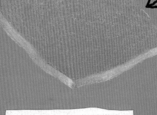

AMERICAN CHEESE

So yec

MUENSTER

Really stinky

and gooey

BRIE

Just smelly

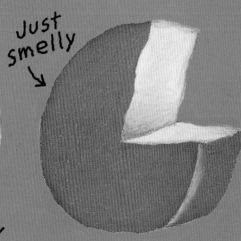

FONTINA

PORT-SALUT

THAT LAY IN THE HOUSE THAT JACK BUILT.

Call Jack for key

THAT ATE
HE CHEESE
THAT
LAY IN
HE HOUSE
THAT
JACK BUILT.

PHEW

Call Jack
for key

THIS IS THE CAT

SPHINX CAT
A hairless cat that looks like a pug dog.

MAINE COON
A very appealing and popular cat.

ALLEY CAT
A mixed breed and very independent.

FELIX
One of the most famous Comix characters.

MANX
A cat without a tail.

SIAMESE CAT
It needs lots of attention and love.

BOMBAY CAT
A very interesting pet with a jet-black coat.

BURMESE CAT
A cat for lovers of little cats.

CAT IN HAT CAT
Goofy behavior - talks in rhyme.

CHESHIRE CAT
A very mysterious cat.

HALLOW
A par tric

KORAT CAT
A cat that brings good luck.

THAT KILLED
THE RAT

Cheddar
99 lb.

THAT
ATE
THE
CHEESE.
THAT
LAY
N THE HOUSE
HAT JACK BULT.

Call Jack
for Key

THAT WORRIED
THE
CAT
KILLED THE
THAT
RAT
THAT ATE THE
CHEESE
THAT LAY
IN THE HOUSE
THAT JACK
BUILT.

Cheddar
99 lb.

Call
Jack
for key

THAT TOSSED THE DOG THAT WORRIED THE CAT THAT ILLED THE RAT THAT ATE THE CHEESE HAT LAY N THE HOUSE HAT JACK BUILT.

MEE OW MEOW

THIS IS THE MAIDEN ALL FORLORN

THIS IS THE ROOSTER THAT CROWED IN THE MOR

The Rooster
by Little Red Hen

When I hear
that awful crow
that is when
I surely know
I am awake
...head to toe

THIS IS THE FARMER PLANTING HIS CORN

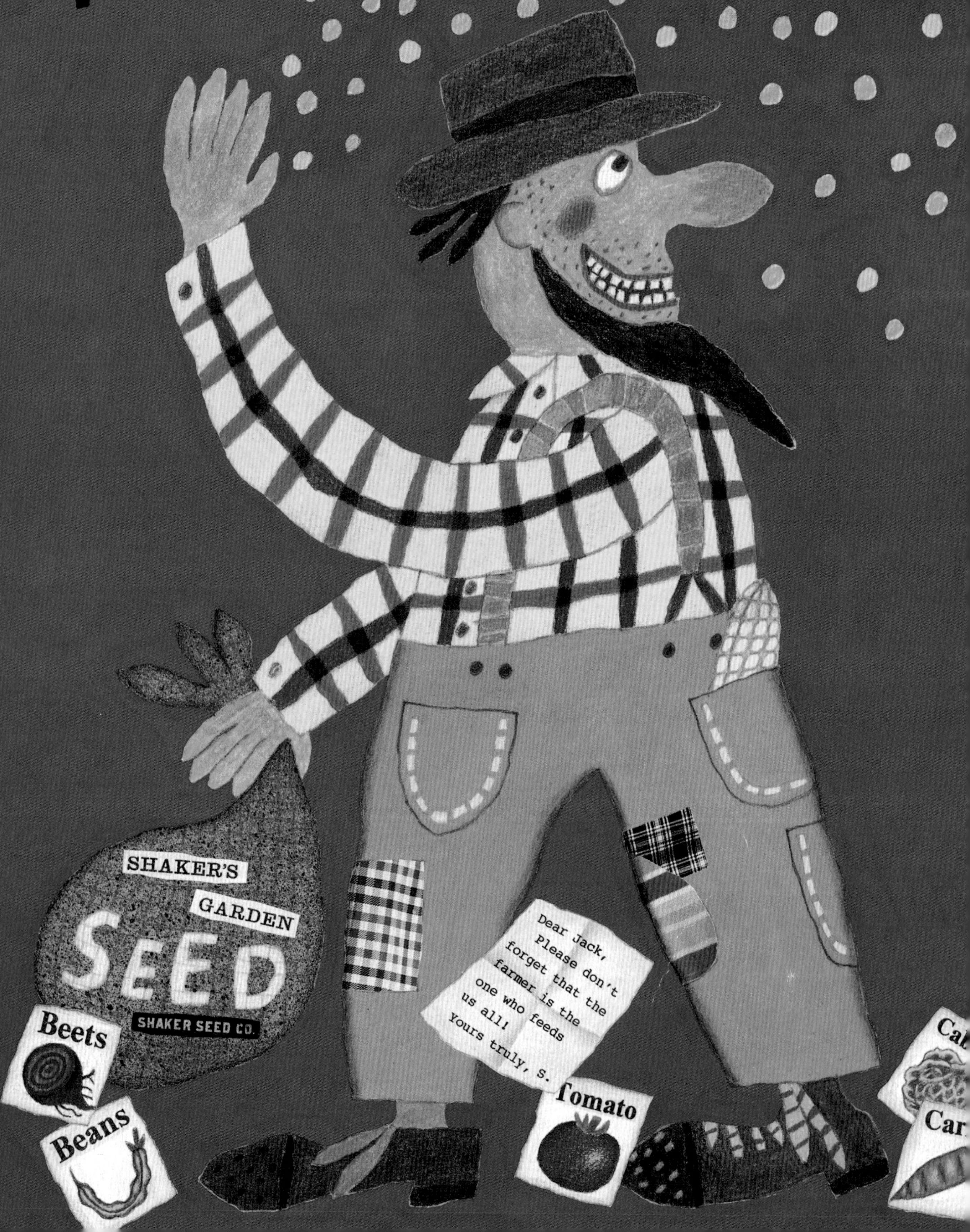

THAT LAY

IN THE HOUSE

THAT JACK

BUILT.

THIS IS THE HOUSE THAT JACK BUILT, a favorite rhyme for children
for several centuries, was first published in 1755 and probably derive
from an ancient Hebrew chant in the 16th century.
It was illustrated by Randolph Caldecott in 1878.

adise Found-beautiful post & beam
. mhse on approx. 51+ magnificent
. Lovely level land w/lrg pond
cked with fish. This 4 BR, 2.5 bth, 2
house is nestled amongst flowering
es, shrubs & perennials. Anderson
ench wood SGD's open to decks in
most every room-truly unique. What
ws! What wildlife abounds! Seen by
ot only. Please call listing agt Ellsa

SIMPLY ELEGANT

Beautifully sited on prime 19 acres in
the heart of Bedford. Glamorous
shingle style 6000+ sf of quality construction. Oversized living room w/fpl.
Enormous gourmet's kitchen. Lavish
master suite w/sitting room, fpl &

STUNNING CONTEMPORARY

Architect designed & set on over 3 acs
of prof'lly landscpd seclusion in Lewisboro. Magnificent dropped LR w/20'
ceil, formal DR, sunlit kit adj solarium
b'fast room which leads to outside liv
spaces & spa. 3 fpls, 2-story office/stu-
dio w/sep entrance. Winter views of

ENTIRE 4 STORY TOWNHSE

w/PRIVATE 1,000 SQ FT GARDEN
Steps to Central Pk, 5th & Madison Ave
shopping. Turn of the century house w/
4BR's, 4 full baths & 2 powder rooms.
Sep maid's quarters or perfect

18th Century Manor House

storically-significant, meticulously-
stored 15-rm brick Georgian on 6+
res. Prof'l kitch, elegant bths, new
echanicals. 19th C caretaker's wing.
sk....................$1,100,000

Architect Designed

On a quiet lane, this spectacular home
faces south and draws wonderful light
overlooking 4 beautiful acres. 2-story
cathedral ceiling center hall; fireplaces

EXTRAORDINARY FARM. Early salt-
box-style house w/scrnd porch, deck,
many improves. 124 rolling acres with
fenced horse pastures, hayfields,
woods. Small barn w/apt above, hug

Palenville Gorgeous Escape. Hdwd fls,
fpl, 3BR, full bsmt, fab sett'g, mins to
Woodstock, state preserve & ski'g.
$97.5K Greene County Rlty

C. 1800 CENTER HALL COLONIAL
00 sf brick. Wide CH with Palladian
ndow. Exquisite detail: 15 rms, 5
cs, 5 baths. Guest house with fplc. 2
ist's studios. 3-car gar. Barn. Shop.
lti-lines & LAN for home profession.
cient trees and organic gardens
erywhere. Long tree-lined drive.
nderful country estate.....$1.185M.

UNDERSTATED ELEGANCE
Located on open Long Island sound
and sited on a gentle rise this gracious
custom blt in 1956, and sits majestically
on 1.3 acres of premier waterfront
property. The unobstructed views encompass Larchmont Harbor, umbrella
point & the sound. The well maintained
interior boasts a large living rm with
fireplace and bay window flanked by
doors to the patio, a

A COUNTRY JEWEL
Fabulous country contemporary with
exquisite gardens & decks galore. 3
BRs, 3 baths & fplc. Totally secluded on
6 acres. Priced to sell quickly. $295,000.

BREATHTAKING "Napa Valley-
esque" views in a secluded, tranquil
setting. Glass & log w/soaring ceilings
& massive stone fplc. 40x40 studio/out-
building. 9+ acres of paradise. $450,000.

COUNTRY QUIET
at this sprawling 6BR, 3.5Bth
. framed by mature trees &
plantings on 1.40acs in de-
ate area & you'll be hooked on
fe. Custom blt for lavish en-
mfortable family living, this
" residence boasts

ATTRACTIVE PRICE
Redecorated decor, refinished firs &
new KIT appliances. Set on almost 5
acre in a most convenient location.
4BDs, 3.5bths, LR w/fpl, DR, KIT w/
breakfast area opens to deck, Master
w/whirlpool bth, lower level Rec room
w/wet bar,

EXTRA SPECIAL
41 Winthrop Dr...One of Riverside's
most desirable streets, renov. Colonial,
state-of-art kitchen & fam. rm, 4BRs,
2.5bths, a/c. CB#GFP5075 ....$1,625,000

SUNDAY 1-3PM
Lovely old & charming Colonial in the
Huntswood area, feat 4BR's, 2 baths
EIK, LR/fpl, hdwd flrs, wond htd prch
new heating systm, 2-car gar & privacy
Near train, bus & shops. $349,500
dir:Cross County Prkwy to Gramatan